REVENGE DOESN'T PAY

REVENGE DOESN'T PAY

Abigail Rose Fucci

Charleston, SC
www.PalmettoPublishing.com

Revenge Doesn't Pay

First Edition

Paperback ISBN: 978-1-63837-692-7

To all our police and detectives that work round the clock
and to all expectant mothers.

Title of Contents

Chapter 1

The loud screams of the phone echoed through my ears. I rolled over in my bed and stole a glance at my bedside clock radio.

"Two in the morning!" I exclaimed out loud. "I wonder who it is at this unearthly hour? Well, I guess I better answer it. I know that whoever it is won't stop calling." After getting out of bed, I picked up the phone.

"Emily, it's Josh! You have to come quick!"

"Josh!" I exclaimed. "What's the matter? It's two in the morning!"

"Something big! Better get over to Blackwell Manor quick, and I mean ASAP! Can't speak over the phone just now, but this is important! I have to hang up now. Sergeant Richards is approaching. See you there!"

"Wait Josh---" but it was too late. He had already hung up. "Well," I thought, "I'd better hurry over." I quickly got out of bed, changed into a sweater, pants, and grabbed my detective kit, which includes a magnifying glass, finger printing set, tape, and other important items.

Once I was ready, I tiptoed past my three dogs.

"Well, that didn't work" I said out loud. I had just noticed my Irish Wolfhound, Rory, lift his head. "Stay boy; I'll be back soon." I slipped quietly downstairs, put on my shoes, and went out the door.

Now, I know what you'll think next. "A horse for means of transportation? Am I crazy or what?" Well, the fact is I do have a car and I use it a lot; however, out here in the great west country, Wyoming, some of us use horses for short distances; also, they don't use gasoline.

So, I saddled my horse, hoisted myself onto the saddle, and galloped off. I looked back at my ranch house, and thought to myself, "This could be the last time I'm here at home." I know this sounds depressing, but it reminds me that life is a gift, and that God is free to take away any of our lives, just as He has given them to us.

I galloped off into the darkness, not knowing what might happen next.

Chapter 2

"Whoa there," I said as I reigned up my mare, Paint. I looked up at Blackwell Manor. Outside around the house seemed cold and dark; however, I could see lights on inside the house.

"I guess I'm the last one here, as usual," I thought to myself. I got off my horse and went inside, shutting the door behind me. "Josh! Hellooo! Anyone home?" I asked, raising my voice.

"Oh, is that you Emily?" Josh asked. "We're in the sitting room." I made my way into the room and observed my surroundings.

It was a huge room with plush carpet that had an Indian design. The furniture was eccentric, with two long comfortable divans on the left side, the center contained a table for tea and to set books on, the two back corners contained cabinets that had various knickknacks, the right side had an elaborate desk and chair for writing letters, and there was a great big chandelier over our heads. Josh and the sergeant were standing while another man, Inspector Carol, who I was not happy to see, sat on one of the divans.

"Well," I said, "What do we have here?"

Sergeant Richards looked in his notes and said, "Thirty-five-year-old Susie Blackwell was found dead in her bed about an hour ago. Her maid discovered her after she thought that she heard a noise come from the bedroom. However, we think she was dead and has been dead for several hours now."

"Has the maid been spoken too? Who else lived with Miss Blackwell?" I inquired.

"No," said Josh. "No one has been interviewed, and there is a butler, a gardener, a cook, and a chauffeur, besides the maid."

"Hey--look fellows, I don't know what you see in this, but it clearly is an open and shut case. No mystery here!" exclaimed Inspector Carol. "She died completely from a heart issue."

"But Miss Blackwell's heart was in perfect condition!" I argued. "That I know for a fact."

"That's true," said Josh. "However, we won't know anything yet until a post-mortem is done on the body. The doctor said he would be here shortly."

"In the meantime," I stated, "we should interview everyone that knew Miss Blackwell for information that might help us."

Sergeant Richards looked on his list and said, "Only the butler, maid, and cook live here; the gardener commutes to work here."

"Okay," I said. "We'll start with the maid." I looked at Josh and he nodded in agreement. I noticed that Inspector Carol had disdain in the look on his face. He obviously wasn't enjoying himself.

"Oh," said Richards, "and what is more baffling is that there's no sign of a struggle and no blood anywhere."

"And that means…" I trailed off, waiting for his response.

"Suicide" he finished. I just shut my eyes and counted to ten. Then I opened them.

"Inspector, please bring in the maid," Josh requested. As soon as the Inspector stood up, we heard a car drive up, the lights went out, and a crash all in that order, leaving us in a total, mysterious darkness.

Chapter 3

Everything was confusion itself! "What was that!?" exclaimed Inspector Carol.

"What's going on out there!?" shouted Sergeant Richards. Josh and I just looked at each other. The door opened, then closed with a bang. Footsteps sounded towards the sitting room.

"Well, I see we're having a night fest here! Why are all the lights off?" asked Dr. Hitchens. Hitchens was a reliable doctor who worked with the police force and Josh knew him well. He was in his fifties, with some graying hair, sideburns, and a beard.

"Oh, we just love sitting in the dark," said Inspector Carol sarcastically. I just rolled my eyes. Honestly, sometimes Inspector Carol really irritated me.

"Actually," I said, "just as you drove up, we all heard a crash and at the same time the lights went out."

"Probably a circuit breaker tripped or something. I'll check it out," offered Josh. He left the room, and meanwhile, Sergeant Richards found candles and lit them.

"So, where is the body?" inquired Dr. Hitchens.

Inspector Carol replied, "Still on the bed asleep, never to wake again...." I saw for a split second an eerie smile on his face, but then it vanished. I wondered what that meant or was he just a completely creepy guy all around. I didn't have time now to figure it out.

"I'll show you the way Doc. Inspector, please wait for Josh. He should be around shortly." After witnessing that expression on Inspector Carol's face, I did not want to be around him, so that is the main reason he was asked to wait for Josh. In addition, the only help Inspector Carol was offering were his corny and ridiculous remarks.

Doc, Sergeant, and I, holding a lighted candle, went up the stairs to the second floor. There were two main bedrooms and four guest bedrooms. Each room had a walk-in closet and adjoining bathroom. Once we reached the top of the stairs, we turned right down a hallway, and entered the first main bedroom we came too. Suddenly, the lights came back on. "Perfect timing Josh," I mumbled.

Susie's pale face was clearly visible. The doctor went over and did a quick look-over at her body. "I'd say," started the doctor, "that she has been dead since 10 pm. I'm not sure about the cause though, it could be suicide or murder or natural causes. I'll have an ambulance pick up her body for a postmortem; then hopefully we'll find out the cause of death. Let's go downstairs now and see about talking to her maid." We left the room, shut the door, and went back downstairs as suggested.

Josh was there and speaking with the maid. The inspector was not in sight. Josh turned to us and spoke up saying, "Inspector Carol left-he said that he had better things to do at 3:30am and that as far as he is concerned, there's no mystery about anything here. In addition, the maid just told me that crash we heard was her dropping some glass."

"Oh," I said. "What about the lights?"

"It seems that someone went to the trouble of turning the main breaker off. Why? I don't know. I don't know who could have done it because we were all up here."

"Hmmm," replied Doc Hitchens. "It seems that we have an intruder in this house, or should I say an unexpected guest. We need to keep a sharp lookout for anything suspicious." The sound of the ambulance drew up to the house. "Oh, that is my cue to exit. After the body is taken away, I'll follow and will let you know my findings asap." Several medics entered with a stretcher. Doc showed them upstairs and they soon came back down with Susie's body. They all went out the door, and the Doc followed.

"Well, let's get down to questioning," said Sergeant Richards.

"Sergeant, it's pretty early in the morning and Emily and I need our sleep," said Josh. Boy was he a life saver!

"All right," replied Richards. "I'll question her myself. You guys get some sleep and meet me here tomorrow morning."

"Sounds good!" said Josh enthusiastically, and I nodded with a tired smile. Then we walked out the door.

Chapter 4

"Ohhh…" I groaned as I rolled over in my bed. "I wonder what time it is?" I asked myself. I looked at my clock and my eyes were wide open at seeing that it was 10am! "Raspberries! I'm going to be late!" I jumped out of bed, changed, brushed my hair, and ran downstairs to grab a bite to eat. My dogs followed me into the kitchen, and I poured out their food and water. Then I opened the front door so they could go outside and do their business. I watched them all file out and I followed.

"Chores," I muttered. "Better get those done before I leave." So, I grabbed a bucket and went out to milk the cows one after the other. Afterwards, I fed the chickens and gathered the eggs. Once that was finished, I checked on the sheep and the horses. I brought in my horse after letting the others out, saddled him up, and went back inside. Rory, Fluffy, and Tipper followed me inside. I stored the eggs, which I had put in egg cartons, in the fridge and poured the milk evenly into jars. Then I put the jars into the fridge-yes, I sell raw milk. I grabbed another bite to eat then walked out the door, shut it, hoisted myself onto the saddle, and rode away.

Upon reaching Blackwell Manor, I realized it was 2pm. "Great," I thought. "Well, I do have a farm to run." Josh came out and grinned.

"Long time no see," he said. "What took you so long? No, wait…don't tell me. You have a farm to run. Sorry, I forgot.

Well, in two weeks, you'll have a husband by your side to help you."

"Thanks a lot," I replied, grinning more than he was. "Okay, but getting serious here, where's Sergeant Richards?"

"He called to say he couldn't make it. We are to go on without him. I thought he'd already asked the maid some questions, but apparently, he didn't. And we should be getting some information soon on how Susie Blackwell died," responded Josh.

"Let's go," I said. We walked into the Manor house and found the maid dusting the furniture. "Sorry to interrupt," I said, "but we'd like to ask you some questions if you don't mind." The maid looked up, then sat down on a chair.

"I suppose," she said, "that you want to know my whereabouts before Susie was found."

"By you?" asked Josh.

"Yes," she said. "I don't know who would want to kill her, and I certainly didn't do it."

"Of course not," said Josh, "but we need to establish everyone's whereabouts, so please answer our questions."

"All right," she said. "Well, as I normally do, I served madam dinner at six in the evening sharp. There was steak with gravy, mashed potatoes, cod, peas, corn, bread pudding, salad, and coffee. I guess it was sort of an addiction, but madam always had coffee with every meal. Anyways, after dinner, Miss Blackwell went into her private den to read and write letters."

There was a pause, and the maid, Clare Thompson, looked uneasy. "Go on," I urged her.

"Well, I don't know if I should tell you this, but madam didn't look to well that day. She always did keep to herself. But that evening, while I was passing by her study, I heard some raised voices-hers and a man's. We had no guests over, and no one came by the front door. So, I wasn't sure who it could be until I heard his name mentioned."

"What is the name that was mentioned?" Josh asked.

"Wilbur Copewell," the maid replied.

"What relation is he to our victim, Miss Blackwell?" I asked.

"He's her ex-boyfriend before she married," the maid answered. "They had some argument about something, and it seemed it would come to blows. So, I knocked and opened the door, and Susie was there alone. But I know I heard him in there. Susie was in a bad mood. She just glared at me, then left the room and went upstairs to her bedroom. She didn't come out and I didn't see her again till I discovered…" Her voice trailed off.

"I see," said Josh. "What did you say about her being married?"

"I never knew that she was married much less engaged," I said, looking puzzled.

"Oh!" exclaimed the maid. "Don't you know? It was quite the scandal when it occurred."

"No," we both replied.

"Well," said the maid, "It seems that some years ago, Miss Blackwell ran off and eloped with a young man named Dick Purcell. They married and the story goes that she had a child, but no one has ever heard or seen the child, if he or she even exists. Well, after several years, they had a fight and he up and left her. Not too long after, Susie started to see Wilbur again."

"So," I said out loud, "Dick Purcell is Susie's estranged husband."

Chapter 5

"**S**o," said the sergeant, who had shown up but was late, "we have two suspects so far-her husband and her boyfriend." I nodded at the maid and, and she left the room.

"So now, all we have to do is track down these two men; it seems so simple" I said sarcastically. "But really, where do we start in our search? We also should speak to the gardener, butler, and the cook. Of course, I doubt it'll shed much light."

"It might," said Josh. "You never know."

"Well," intervened the sergeant, "I'll have a chat with our friends here, you know, the butler, cook, and gardener, and you two can tackle Dick and Wilbur."

"Just peachy," I thought to myself. Josh seemed fine with it, so Richards got up and left to start his interrogations.

"Well!" exclaimed Josh. "I'll go see what information I can dig up on Wilbur, and you can work on Dick." I said yes, got up, and left after saying goodbye to Josh. I jumped on my horse and rode off.

When I got home, I quickly let the dogs out and checked up on the animals. Then I went inside to find Dick's address and profile. Yes, in case you're wondering, I have ways of finding out information that I need. "Nothing much on him," I said out loud. I found his address and decided to go pay him a visit. I changed into jeans and a sweater and got into my SUV. I remembered fortunately to have pepper spray in case I'd need it. I set my GPS, then thought I'd better bring Rory along just for assurance of my safety. So, I got out, went back inside, fetched Rory, and put him in the back of my SUV. Then, I drove off.

An hour later, I pulled into Dick's, or Mr. Purcell's driveway. I jumped as the ringing of the cell phone started. I answered it saying, "Hello?"

"Emily, it's Josh!"

"What's wrong? You seem quite tense," I told him.

"Well," he said, "I've just had word from the postmortem done on Miss Blackwell."

"And…?" I asked, urging him on.

"She was poisoned by ingesting conium maculatum."

"Poison Hemlock!?" I exclaimed. "How?"

"I'm not sure," replied Josh, "but that's what we need to find out. Oh, I must go now. Talk to you later. Bye."

I hung up the phone and wondered how poison hemlock ended up in her stomach. Maybe it was in her food or something. Then it clicked in my head. "Wait!" I said out loud. "She had salad for dinner and from what I know, had it other days too. It could've been put in her salad, and she thought it was Queen Anne's Lace and ate it. Now the question is who did it and why." I decided that I would tell Josh about it tomorrow. Right now, I needed to question Mr. Purcell. I left the window open a bit for Rory and left the passenger door unlocked. I rang the doorbell and waited. The door opened, and a man of about 36 years old, blonde hair and beard and surprisingly green eyes, stood before me.

"Yeah? What do you want?"

"Mr. Purcell," I said, "I'm here because I want to ask you some questions about Susie Blackwell, your estranged wife." He just stared at me, then let me in.

"Sit down," he said.

"So, what terms were you on with your wife recently?" I asked.

"We never spoke to each other and haven't these past several years. We married young and were very foolish. However, when she was 26 and I was 28, I left her and filed for a divorce. Why? Because I found out that she was being unfaithful and seeing another man!"

"Wilbur Copewell?" I asked.

"Yes," he said. "She wouldn't divorce me at first, but then something changed her mind and she complied. We hadn't spoken to each other since then."

"What about the child?" I asked.

"Child? What child? We had no child. I have a condition that doesn't allow me to, well, you know..."

"Hmmm," I said, "then the child must be..."

"Her and Wilbur's," he finished.

"Where were you the day Miss Blackwell died?" I asked.

"Why do you ask?" he countered. He stood up, and so did I.

"Mr. Purcell, we must establish everyone's whereabouts, so please answer the question."

"Are you saying I'm a suspect!? You have no right to ask me all these questions!" shouted Mr. Purcell. He started forward and soon had me pinned against the wall. "I must ask you to leave right now!"

"Please! Mr. Purcell, back away! You are crossing my boundaries!" I exclaimed. He kept inching closer and closer till I could stand it no longer and I screamed like crazy! He covered my mouth, so I did whatever I could think of. I bit him, and hard. He cursed, drew his hand away, and then I pushed him away with all my might. He grabbed me, and just then the door burst open! In bounded Rory, and to my great surprise, Josh!

Chapter 6

"**S**mack!" And down went Mr. Purcell in a heap with Rory growling on top of him.

"You got here just in time! How'd you know I was in trouble?" I asked.

He kissed me, then said, "I didn't. However, when I saw on Purcell's profile that he has these fits of rage and passion, and gets angry easily, I was worried about your safety. After I had interviewed Wilbur, I came over here as quickly as possible, and let Rory out on the way in."

"Wow!" I said. "Great timing!"

"He didn't hurt you I hope?"

"No," I replied, "and thank goodness for that."

"I'll get you for this!" exclaimed Mr. Purcell, as he was getting up off the ground. Rory growled at him and cornered him against the wall. "Get this blasted beast away from me!" Purcell screamed.

"Quiet, Rory!" I said. "That's enough. You know, I could have you arrested and charged with assault, Mr. Purcell. However, since I don't want to trouble either of us, I won't."

"Come on," said Josh. "We'd better leave before he blows his cork at us." Then he whispered, "Can we discuss the case at your place?"

"Not now," I replied. "I have something to do, but how about tomorrow night, and maybe we should invite Sergeant Richards over so we can all discuss the case."

"Sounds good. I'll let him know." We both, along with Rory, left the house, got into our own cars, and drove away.

That night, I could barely sleep. The occurrences of the day kept rolling over in my mind. Finally, I drifted off to sleep. The next day was a busy one. A couple of farm hands and I got our produce ready for market. I made sure that the meats and veggies were aboard. The whole day was uneventful, but was successful. Evening finally came, and I made sure the table was set for three. I had prepared some pot roast hash and mashed potatoes with chocolate pie for dessert. Everything seemed to be ready. My dogs had already had their dinner. So, I sat down on the sofa, and reviewed the notes I had written about the case.

The doorbell rang and I went to answer it. "Oh, hey guys! Come on in. I was just reviewing the case."

Richards sat down on the rocking chair with a quizzical expression on his face. He said, "Josh tells me she died from poison hemlock. How on earth could that have happened?" Josh just sat down in the armchair across from Richards, and just stared at me, waiting for me to answer.

"Salad," I said. "But before we talk further, let's eat first."

"Sure," they both said. We all went over and I served the food. After we had eaten and the dishes were cleared, we went back to discuss the case.

"So," Richards said, "You think it was in her salad for that day and the day before?"

"Yes," I said. "She would have to have had it for about one to two days. As you know, she probably thought it was Queen Anne's Lace, which is edible and commonly mistaken for poison hemlock."

"All right," said Josh. "That's the 'how,' but what about the 'who' and the 'why'?"

"Well," said Richards, "Purcell could've done it. He seems to have a motive. As her estranged husband, he could've been jealous when she started to see Wilbur. They could've argued, and in a fit of rage, decided to do away with her. So, as not to be detected too easily, he concocted a brilliant way to murder her-put poison hemlock in her salad; he could've snuck in without anyone knowing and put it in there."

"Maybe," I said, unsure, "but that's a weak motive. It could've been Wilbur, and for the same reasons, or maybe even reasons unknown currently."

"Or," said Josh, "the culprit could be person or persons unknown. Maybe a sibling, although I doubt it. Maybe that child that's supposedly living. He or she could have been upset at the way she was living and killed her."

"I believe we should delve deeper," I said. "Oh, Josh, what did Wilbur have to say?"

"Oh," he sighed, "not much. He pretty much denied killing her, didn't know what hemlock was, and claimed he had been head over heels in love with Susie. He also claimed that he was at home the whole time and during the time of her death; however, he has no witnesses."

"I think," said Richards, "that we should start a search for her child. It could be a good lead."

"Well, I guess so," replied Josh.

"How old would the child be?" I asked.

"About 18 years old," Richards stated.

Just then the phone rang. I got up and answered it. "Hello?" I said.

"Emily, it's me Rachel."

"Oh, hey Rachel, what's up?"

"I think I got some important info to tell you about Susie's death."

"Oh? What is it?" I inquired.

"I can't say over the phone, but please, can you come over to my place tomorrow, along with Josh and the other person-Richards?"

19

"Sure," I said. "Excited for the wedding?"

"I sure am!" she exclaimed. "Oh!!" There was a gasp on the other end.

"What's going on? Rachel? Hello!?"

"I've got to go now," she replied shakily. "I think I'm being watched, or maybe even listened too. Bye." Then I heard a resounding click on the other end.

Chapter 7

"What happened?" asked Josh.

"Yes, tell us!" exclaimed Richards.

"I'm not sure," I replied. "It was Rachel, and she said that she had important information to help us but couldn't say anything over the phone. Then, all of a sudden, she said that someone was watching her. Then she hung up."

"Well, should we go over and see what's up?" inquired Josh.

"I don't know, since she asked for all of us to come over tomorrow. Maybe Richards could stop by and check on her?" I asked hopefully.

"Sure," he said. "I'll leave now, and let you know tomorrow what's up. Thanks for dinner." Then he got up and left.

"Finally, we're all alone," said Josh. "Forget the case now, and let's talk about us and our wedding."

"Okay," I said. "I could sure use a break. I sent out all the invitations and everyone, surprisingly, said they'd come."

"That's good," he said. He scooched over next to me and then said, "I have to leave actually; sorry I just realized it, but let me kiss my future bride goodnight?" he sort of asked with a smile. I smiled back and nodded. Then he leaned closer, put his arms around my waist and back of my head, and pressed his lips into mine. Then he pulled back and got up.

"Wow!" I said enthusiastically. He grinned, got on his shoes and hat, and walked out the door.

That night, I again had a fitful sleep, wondering why Rachel had hung up so suddenly. After about two hours, I fell asleep. I woke up the next morning to the buzzing of my alarm clock and the ringing of the phone at the same time. I quickly got out of bed, turned off the alarm, and then picked up the phone.

"Emily, Richards here-just letting you know I stopped over at Rachel's last night. Everything seemed fine." His voice sounded tense.

"And..." I prodded.

"Well, she seemed fine, but when I asked her what was bothering her, she said nothing was, vehemently denied it, and then actually opened the door for me to leave. Well, so I took my cue but said that I would be back. And here I am calling you from home. I'm about to leave for work. Are you still in for tonight?"

"Yes," I said. "I'm concerned and believe we should definitely go."

"Okay, see you later." Then, he hung up. I laid back down in bed, then forced myself out of bed. I got dressed and went downstairs to feed the dogs and do the farm chores.

Later that day, I decided to drive to Rachel's a little earlier than planned. I got there and went up the walkway. I knocked but received no answer. I tried the door, and it was unlocked, so I let myself in. The house seemed unusually quiet. "Rachel!" I shouted. No answer. I ran throughout the house-upstairs, downstairs, everywhere. I was puzzled; then, I went back upstairs and found her bedroom door shut and bolted. I knocked-no response. I was worried. Then I heard footsteps coming up, and there appeared Josh and Richards.

"Something's gone wrong," I said. "She won't answer."

"We'll break down the door," said Richards.

"One, two, three," both said and rammed against the door with their bodies. It broke open and we all rushed in! I gasped at what I saw and put my hand to my heart.

22

Chapter 8

"**R**achel!" I cried. I rushed over to her and knelt down. "She's dead," I said shakily. Richards and Josh just stared.

"Are you sure?" asked Josh.

"Yes," I replied. "But how? Who? Why?" I looked at Josh imploringly.

"Don't worry, Emily," said Richards with a strained voice. "We'll find out who did this." I got up and stared at her. There was a puddle of blood next to her head which was all bashed in. The blood had poured out of her head.

"Better call the police and ambulance," remarked Josh. He went off and made the calls. I covered up Rachel's body with a sheet and then left the room. I went downstairs with Richards following me. After we got down, I turned and again asked why. Richards said nothing; instead, he went outside to search for clues. Meanwhile, Josh came back, and the police and ambulance arrived. Josh opened up the door and showed the EMTs upstairs while the police started an investigation.

"There's not much to go on, but we'll try our best. We didn't pick up any fingerprints; the murderer must have worn gloves," informed the lieutenant. The EMTs came down with Rachel's body on a stretcher. They carried her out into the ambulance. The police surgeon came over and looked grave but puzzled.

"He said, "The crime had to have been committed with a hard weapon, something where one to two smashes on the head could kill someone. But there's no weapon near the body, so the culprit must have disposed of it somewhere and somehow." Then he said good day and left.

After they'd all gone, Richards rushed in and exclaimed, "I believe I found the weapon that was used!"

"Where is it?" both Josh and I asked. Richards produced a good-sized hammer with some good-sized blood stains.

"That has to be it, but who would be so brutal as to do such a cruel thing?" I asked.

"Someone who didn't want her to say anything about what she knew of Susie's death. Could've been the person who was watching her," said Richards.

"It must've been someone she knew," claimed Josh.

"How so?" I asked.

"Well, she was found in her bedroom, so she must have known the person; they went up to her room together and when Rachel turned her back towards the person, he or she must have struck."

"Maybe," I said, "but it could've been a stranger who asked her to get something, followed her up, and then struck her."

"We really have multiple possibilities," added Richards.

"That's true. I guess we need more evidence before we point fingers," I mentioned.

"Definitely," replied Richards.

"I think we should take apart both murders, find a motive, figure out our suspects, and research this eighteen-year-old child of Susie's," remarked Josh.

"How on earth do we go about finding her child?" I asked.

"Search all nearby hospitals," replied Josh, "and search for birth certificates."

"I'll look into that end," said Richards.

"Ok," I said, "and I'll check up on suspects."

"I'll help you," insisted Josh with a grin.

"Then let's split," I said, "and meet again within a week." We all went downstairs, with the hammer, and went our own ways. I had to go back home and tend to the farm, then go to bed.

The next day, after checking on the animals, I decided to start researching our suspects and their backgrounds. I spent one day on each-Purcell and Copewell. Then I decided to write down the motives and of course, I reasoned how and when and everything to the last detail. "Well," I said out loud, "In relation to Susie's death, Purcell could've done it out of jealousy and revenge. However, Copewell could've also done it, maybe out of spite or jealousy, even anger, since it is known he had an argument with her before she died. Then again, it could've been her unknown child, or an unknown person. I believe that Purcell was holding information back. The question is-why?" I pondered all this the whole week. I knew that if we figured out the first murder, we'd have our answer for the second. I hoped that Richards and Josh were having better luck than I was.

Chapter 9

It was a cold, windy day, and the clip-clop of my horse's hooves was all that could be heard. I was taking Paint out for a ride to clear my brain. It had been over a week, and I was still attempting to crack the case. As a matter of fact, it was over two weeks since the whole case opened up. Even longer than that-the problem that I have is whenever a case opens up, I lose track of time. So, it could be a few weeks and I won't have noticed for a while because I become completely wrapped up in these murder investigations. Anyways, I had just gone to Mass on Sunday, and delayed work till Monday. As everyone knows, or as most of you all know, Sunday is the sabbath and a day of rest.

The cool fresh breeze was inviting. I steered my mount around and back to the farm. It was time to start work again, and I actually had ideas this time. I returned home, set Paint out to pasture, and went inside. I sat down on the sofa with a blanket, notebook, pencil, and my three dogs curled up around me. I was in the middle of writing down ideas when pieces started to fall in place. The picture, though vague and faded, was starting to form. I jumped at the sound of the phone ringing.

"Hello?" I said into the phone.

"Do I have news for you!" boomed a voice.

"Richards?" I asked, amused that he didn't introduce himself. I realized that he must have made some breakthrough.

"Yeah, it's me," he replied.

"What is it? More info?" I inquired.

"Yes," he said. "I picked up a lot of interesting information. However, I've been working all day and night, and it took me awhile to dig everything up, but I've finally figured out some of the missing puzzle pieces."

"Well, don't stop there and keep me waiting in suspense," I said eagerly.

"Well, here it goes. Susie Blackwell gave birth to a baby girl when she was 17, but before she married Dick Purcell. However, Dick is the father. But Ms. Blackwell didn't let Dick know about the baby and kept it quiet and a secret by putting the baby up for adoption. Dick contracted an STD after having married her. I went through some medical records that showed Susie had gotten an STD, presumably from being with Wilbur for a time after having her baby. She then breaks up with Wilbur, and goes back to Dick, this time marrying him. Now he can't do his part to procreate, and because of this awareness of his STD, he is unaware of the daughter he has currently. Or at least I think he is unaware-I could be wrong about that. She is 18 and her name is Lila Burns. She is a possible suspect in this case." Richards took a deep breath, then breathed out.

"Wow!" I exclaimed. "You sure did your research. So, should we track down this Lila Burns?"

"Already did that," he replied. "She lives with her adopted parents, a Brendan and Sylvia Rogers at 1325 Sycamore Avenue."

"Did you visit her?" I asked.

"Not yet, but you could have a girl to girl talk with her, and if she doesn't believe you on any of this, then show her the birth certificate which you can get at my office."

"I'll do that," I sighed. "Then once I've met her, we can figure out a plan on who our prime suspect is, and then lay a trap.

Oh! I think I'm getting an incoming call. Bye now." I hung up, and shortly afterwards, the phone rang again. "Hello?" I said into the phone.

"Emily, it's Josh. I've been trying to reach you for 20 minutes."

"I'm sorry Josh, but I was speaking with Richards. What's wrong?" I asked.

"Lots," he replied. "Wilbur Copewell is dead. Stabbed in the back. Now what do you make of that?"

"Oh my!" I exclaimed, shocked. "Where are you now?"

"At his house," Josh said.

"I'll be there shortly," I assured him, and hung up. How could this happen? What was the motive? One thing was for sure-I needed to meet this Lila Burns, and fast, before someone else turned up dead. I got ready, then headed out the door. I jumped into my SUV and drove off.

Chapter 10

After arriving at the house, I let myself in. A spooky feeling crept through my body and shivers ran down my spine. I shook it off and walked through, calling out Josh's name. Nothing. "That's odd," I thought. "He should be here." All of a sudden, a moan sounded nearby. I followed the sound to the kitchen and gasped-Josh was lying down on the floor unconscious! I knelt down and rubbed his wrists, then patted his cheeks. Slowly, he stirred, then opened his eyes.

"What happened?" he asked, looking confused.

"I don't know. You tell me," I said.

"Oh, now I remember, I came to the kitchen for a drink of water. Next thing I know, something hard hit me on the head, and I blacked out."

"Well, somebody sure is nervous and probably thinks we're coming close to the truth," I remarked. "Who do you think is responsible for all this?" Josh stood up slowly.

"My bet is on Lila Burns. But now I'll take you to see the body. The paramedics should be arriving shortly to collect the body." We both walked to the living room where Copewell's body was on the floor.

"So, Richards told you about Burns?" I asked.

"Yes, before he told you. She seems so mysterious. No one has ever seen her, yet she does exist." Josh seemed a bit perplexed.

I looked down and stared at Copewell's body. "Well, who-ever it is sure has guts to kill like that and must have really disliked him. It could be Lila Burns, I guess, but let's not forget about Mr. Purcell. I don't think any one of Susie's servants had a hand in any of the murders. They are all too faithful." I stared at the body for a bit more, then walked toward the front door waiting for the paramedics and doctor to arrive.

Sirens could be heard, and before I could count to five, the paramedics showed up and came into the house. I showed them to the living room, and the doctor first examined the body. The police also showed up, taped off the whole area outside the house, went around with their routine check-up, and after taking statements from us, they left. Two officers stayed behind to guard the place.

The doctor finally stood up and grimaced. He then stated, "This killer is a vicious one, showing no mercy, and that's one of the worst kinds."

"Why do you say that?" asked Josh.

"Well, look closely at the stab wounds. These penetrations shows that the killer repeatedly stabbed him. Then to make sure he wasn't still alive, he or she after the last stabbing stuck the knife into him and twisted it hard. Cruel. So cruel."

"Wow!" I muttered. I couldn't believe someone would do that, and after seeing all sorts of crimes and bodies in my prac-tice, I was still in shock! The doctor left the house, shaking his head and muttering under his breath. Josh and I just looked at each other and watched the paramedics take away the body.

"Three murders," remarked Josh, "and no concrete evidence."

"Except for the weapons," I said, "but we have to keep trying before anything else happens." I furrowed my brow. "If only we had something incriminating, maybe some incriminating evidence. We don't know what motive Lila Burns could have if she is the culprit."

"Maybe," said Josh, "we should try to find her and that way we could talk to her. I've been thinking though, how is it that her last name is different from her biological and adopted parents' last names?"

I shrugged. "She could have changed her name or gotten married, although she is 18. It's possible."

Josh frowned; then he exclaimed, "I know! I'll call Richards up and ask to see if he could help us check Church and court records of marriages recently. Maybe there is one for her." Josh quickly called up Richards and asked if he could help discover if there was a marriage involving a Lila Blackwell, Lila Purcell, or a Lila Rogers.

"I'll get on it right away," promised Richards.

After Josh hung up, he smiled. "We are finally getting somewhere," he said. I smiled back and we walked outside of Copewell's house.

Chapter 11

I was back at home again and doing farm chores. While collecting eggs, milking cows, sending horses out to pasture, and everything else that occurs on a farm, my brain was trying to piece the puzzle of this whole mess together. After I finally finished the chores, I went inside, whipped up some lunch, and sat down with a pen and notebook.

I wrote down a list of our victims, possible suspects, and potential motives. I experimented around and finally came to a conclusion. I had decided that Lila Burns might have married young, that her adopted parents raised her and may or may not have told Lila what they knew about her biological parents, and that she must be our killer. "Women can be vicious killers," I said aloud. Then, I figured that she killed her mom for the way she treated her father and for getting rid of her. Of course, she had to have found out who her parents were and everything about them somehow. Then she killed Wilbur for being a drunken loser and for being with her mom. Finally, Rachel had to die because she must have discovered something important about Susie's death.

I looked at what I had written, then realized that I had accidentally switched Wilbur's and Rachel's deaths. I drew arrows to swap them back and then thought, "Wait, if she is married, then the information about where and who she lives with is fake. If it's not fake, then maybe that address is old and she moved somewhere else with her husband. Or, that could be the proper address but she lives with her husband and not her adopted parents." I realized that I would have to visit the address given to find out just who lived there.

I looked at my motives, then thought again of the culprits. "Well," I started out loud, "it might have been Dick Purcell. He could have done the same thing as Lila, except that he would have killed his wife and Wilbur because he was cheated on." Then I gasped. "Wait!" I exclaimed. "What if Lila teamed up with her father Dick, and he is protecting her. In addition, maybe he lied about not knowing who Lila is and who knows if he really has an STD."

That last thought just blew my mind. I knew I needed to get down to Richard's office fast and call up Josh to tell him to meet me there. I quickly got ready, let out the dogs, left a message on Josh's cell since he didn't pick up, let the dogs back in, grabbed my keys, and drove off. The traffic was pretty intense and I was a little impatient-time was slipping by right through my fingers. I waited and slowly inched forward. Soon, we finally started moving. As soon as I arrived at Richard's office, I parked, got out, and rushed up the stairs into the building and impatiently waited for the elevator. After I entered, I pressed for the 10th floor and waited. Once I got there, I rushed out and burst into Richard's office! My jaw dropped wide open.

"Well, look who finally got here!" exclaimed Richards.

"Yeah, gosh! What took you so long?" inquired Josh teasingly. I just stared at him.

"How did you get here so quickly?" I asked surprised. "I just left a message on your cell."

"Well," he grinned, "I was already on my way when you called. So, I guess I had a head start."

"Did you at least get my message on your cell?"

"It didn't come by carrier pigeon," Richards joked. I stared at him and frowned. "Okay, sorry. Bad joke," he apologized.

"Pathetic," said Josh, "but yes, I did get your message Emily."

"So, tell us your theory," interrupted Richards.

"After going through several theories of what could have happened," I began as I took a seat, "I pounced on a totally new and logical one. Lila could be married-no, let's say she is married and lives with her husband. Then she wouldn't really be with her adopted parents. Maybe she doesn't even live at that address. Well, she could have collaborated with her father and together they could have put an end to Susie, Rachel, and Wilbur. If not, he might actually know she committed these crimes and is protecting her."

"Which means that he lied to us when he mentioned that he didn't know a Lila Burns," replied Richards.

"Exactly," I said.

"It is worth investigating," said Josh.

"Well, I may be able to clear up one angle for you," remarked Richards.

"Oh, what's that?" I asked.

"I did lots of researching, endless researching, and found out that Lila did get married. It was a private wedding, and guess who the two witnesses were?"

"Who?" I asked with anticipation.

"Rachel and her father, Dick Purcell."

"What!?" Josh and I both shouted.

"What is this young man's name? I mean whom did she marry?" inquired Josh.

"A Mr. Robert Burns," replied Richards. "And they live at 35 Elmswood Crest Drive."

"Hmm, looks like you might be on to something Emily," stated Josh.

"One of us should visit her," I said.

"Yeah, and I vote for Emily," Richards remarked.

"Me too," chimed Josh.

"Fine," I said. "I'll go first thing tomorrow." I got up, said goodbye, and left. My brain whirled at the prospect of this new and exciting information.

Chapter 12

As I sat outside on my front porch sipping a cup of hot coffee and watching my dogs frolick around with each other, I was trying to figure out what I would say to Mrs. Burns or what to expect. "Well, time to get going," I muttered. I got up and went inside to get ready for this little excursion that I was getting myself into. I called in my dogs, then grabbed some papers, including Lila's marriage and birth certificates. I then got into my car, and drove off. My brain was in a whirl with all the possible outcomes this visit might bring.

When I finally pulled into the driveway, I realized I felt slightly nervous. I stared up at the huge two-story rambling brick structure. "Gosh! Her husband must be awfully rich for them to own a house like this," I mused aloud. I got out of my car and walked up the driveway and sidewalk to the door. I lifted the huge brass knocker and let it fall hard against the door with a reverberating sound. I stepped back, took a deep breath, and waited.

The door was opened by an elderly man who looked like he could be the manservant or butler.

"Hello? What can I do for you miss?" he asked.

"I would like to see Mrs. Burns please."

"Please come in and wait here." I stepped inside and wondered at the marvel of everything I saw. It was grand but also homey. I wondered just who Lila's husband was. "Miss," said the butler as he came back, "follow me." He then preceded to lead me into a comfortable and cozy living room. "Mrs. Burns will be here shortly." He then left and I just awed at everything I saw. The plush carpet was extremely soft. There was a quaint rocking chair in one corner, bookshelves, a chandelier, coffee table, and two divans. I turned as I heard footsteps coming from the doorway.

"Mrs. Burns?" I inquired.

"Yes, what do you want?" The young woman came in and stood before me. She was very beautiful, had fair skin, dark black wavy hair that reached down right past her shoulders, and her smile seemed as if it could light up the room.

"Surely, this can't be our murderer," I thought. "Then again, looks can be deceiving," I reminded myself.

"I just wanted to ask you some questions regarding, well, your parents." I stared and waited.

"Won't you please sit down," she replied in a soft voice. We both sat down; then I began.

"Perhaps I should introduce myself. I am Emily Randall, a private detective. Myself, and a few others, have been looking into three suspicious deaths: Susie Blackwell, my best friend Rachel Kendricks, and Wilbur Copewell." I paused and looked up. The young lady just put her head down. Then I continued, "We have pinpointed our main suspects; so, I guess you know why I'm here." Lila frowned. She got up, paced the room, then sat down again.

"Please continue," she said.

"Well, it seems that we have two strong suspects with clear motives. Our other one is a Mr. Dick Purcell." I looked at Lila to see her reaction, and to my surprise, her face turned deathly pale.

"My father?!" she gasped. "But why? How? He must be innocent! I know he is!"

"That's easier said than proven," I replied. "Why don't you tell me everything you know."

"Well," she said, "I can tell you that I know he is innocent and so am I! I would never kill my mother, even though I disliked her-a lot."

"I didn't say either of you are guilty for sure; it is just that all the evidence and facts seem to point to you. However, I personally don't believe you did it."

Lila looked somewhat relieved, but still tense. "Well, I was raised by adopted parents who told me what they knew. I figured out myself who my parents were after some tough research, and have been in a close relationship with my dad for some time." She stopped there. Before I could say anything, the front door opened and closed, and footsteps sounded towards the living room.

Chapter 13

I whipped around, startled, then relaxed as I realized that it was only Mr. Burns. He frowned as he entered the room.

"What's going on here!?" he boomed. I judged him to be around 25. His wife just looked at him imploringly.

"Ms. Randall is just here to ask some questions about some mysterious deaths," answered Lila. I just smiled at Mr. Burns.

"Well then, continue questioning!" he boomed. "We have nothing to hide!" I turned back to Lila.

"So, from what you told me, you have a good relationship with your dad, but you disliked your mom and Mr. Copewell." I looked at her, waiting for her response.

"Yes," she said, "but I actually hated my mother. She had no right to do what she did!"

"Well then, where were you at the times of these three murders?" I inquired. Seemed like this could be motive enough for killing her mother.

"Darling, you don't have to answer any of Ms. Randall's questions," interrupted Mr. Burns.

"Let me warn you," I said tensely, "that while you have a right not to answer any questions, it's in your best interest to do so. You have a strong motive. You had means and time. It could easily have been you who killed your mom, Rachel, and Copewell."

"But I didn't kill them! I swear it!" she exclaimed, almost in tears.

"I may believe you're innocent, but what do you think the police will say?" I pressed.

Mr. Burns came over and sat down next to his wife. "We were together all evening," he said, "during her mom's death."

"Really?" I asked. "Can you prove it?"

"No," he said. But his wife looked at him, then at me.

"Yes, we can," she said. "We have to tell the truth," she implored her husband. He nodded. "We were at my father's house. He left, said he had to do something, but he came back about an hour later."

"Do you know where he went?" I asked. She shook her head. "Then, conceivably, he could have gone over to his ex-wife's house, planted the poison hemlock in place of Queen Anne's Lace, and then left," I concluded.

"Maybe," Lila said, "but I know he didn't kill her. We all may have hated her but none of us killed her or the other two for that matter."

"Ok," I sighed. "However, I must tell you that it's just a matter of time before the police arrest someone. It could be you or your father. If they ask any questions, only answer what you can. Not answering may be more incriminating for you." Both of them nodded. I stood up to leave and made my way to the door.

"Goodbye Ms. Randall," said Mr. Burns. He held open the door and I left. As soon as I got home, I called up Josh.

"Hello!" exclaimed Josh.

"Hey darling! It's Emily," I said.

"Oh, what's on your mind?" he inquired.

"Well, I just had a lovely conversation with Lila and her husband."

"Well, good for you! What happened?" he asked.

"Let's just say that I know Lila Burns is innocent, and her husband is too."

"Emily, what about her father?"

"We'll have to check on him some more," I said. "I believe he might be innocent, but I'm not positively sure about it at the moment."

"Would you like me to check up on Dick Purcell for you?" asked Josh.

"Oh, yes! Would you, please?"

"More than happy too," he responded.

"Ok, bye now," I said. After hanging up, I stood lost in thought for a few minutes. Then, I looked around and started my chores. The farm needed tending.

Chapter 14

Preparations were well under way for my wedding. As a matter of fact, the day of my wedding was at hand. In the midst of all the tragedy that had been taking place, Josh and I were not going to delay our wedding anymore. We both decided that we would stick with our jobs for now, and live on the farm that I owned. I couldn't believe that we were finally going to be husband and wife! I was nervous, excited, jittery— it was a dream come true, but still reality.

I was in the bridal room with my few close friends as my bridesmaids, and Agatha, who was my maid of honor. Rachel was supposed to be my maid of honor, but since her murder, I knew that option was no longer an option. Agatha was another close friend. Besides, I was to be married at St. Agatha's anyways.

"You are simply beautiful!" exclaimed Agatha. I just smiled. My long-sleeved white dress, simple but elegant, touched the floor. It sparkled and glittered in the sunlight, and the top half had an embroidered design on it. The veil had been my mother's, who died a few years ago, and had our family crest on it. My bouquet of flowers had quite a few white lilies. I was staring into space when Agatha's voice interrupted my thoughts abruptly.

"Earth to Emily! Wake up!" she exclaimed jokingly.

"Oh!" I exclaimed startled. "Sorry, I must have been day dreaming."

"You were," she said. "It's time for you to walk down that aisle."

We all left the bridal room. I could hear the music playing and could see all the people that were there. My adrenaline was really pumping up and down, and my heart felt as if it would fall out. I was that nervous! I said a Hail Mary, then went to the aisle and started on down. I could just see Josh's face and his radiant smile. Seeing that calmed me down a good deal.

Once I had walked all the way down the aisle, I handed my bouquet to Agatha, then joined hands with Josh. We took our places and faced the direction of the altar and the priest. I looked up at the crucifix, and it seemed that Jesus up on that cross, was smiling down at me. There was going to be a Mass and I have to say that I was excited about all of it! The priest, Fr. Charles Hedgeway, was now at the cathedra (his chair). Mass had started. Everything seemed to go by too quickly. Soon it was time for the vows. Josh and I seriously meant what we said, what we vowed. "Till death do us part" has always been something I remember. It was official once we said the vows, put the rings on each other's fingers, and were pronounced "man and wife."

I smiled when I heard the priest say, "You may now kiss the bride." Of course, Josh did just that. He grabbed my arms, pulled me close, put his hands on my back and the back of my head, and put his lips to mine. That moment was just so relaxing, but it only lasted a moment. I knew there would be more to come. Receiving Jesus in the Eucharist is something that is so amazing—I can't explain it in words and it was amazing during the wedding and Mass. Being at Josh's side and receiving the Host was a bonus!

The ceremony was over before I knew it. Afterwards, there were pictures, maybe too many pictures were taken-I'm not a fan of that many pictures. Finally, everyone headed to the reception. Meanwhile, Josh and I went over to the nearby Mary statue and placed the bouquet of flowers there. We said a silent prayer, then headed over to the reception. I realized that my new life with Josh had just begun.

Chapter 15

Unfortunately, our honeymoon was cut short. We had saved up and traveled to Brazil. It was supposed to have been three weeks but after one and a half weeks, Josh got a call about our case. I know he felt badly about leaving Brazil and cutting short our honeymoon, but it couldn't be helped.

"Darling, you know that I love you! I don't want to leave early from our honeymoon, but—" he broke off, looking upset.

"It's okay honey; I understand. I'm also eager to continue our work on this case." I smiled and he grinned.

"I'm glad," he replied. "We'll leave tomorrow morning." We enjoyed the rest of our day packing and sightseeing.

The next morning, we flew back home—this time, under the same roof as husband and wife. When we arrived home, I started to unpack everything. In case you are wondering where we are living, or if you have forgotten, I'll tell you. Josh and I moved to the farm that I was already living on. He had put his small house up for sale and it sold right after we married. So, we now lived on the farm, and I was unpacking, sorting through mail, listening to phone messages, and much more. Plus, I had to make sure the bank and several other companies had my married name down and his name. This took several weeks, and while I did that, Josh went back to work. I also was wondering about our case and thinking about who the killer might be. I couldn't help but think that it was someone I knew.

Shortly after we had settled in, I received a call from Mr. Purcell. I was shocked, wondering why he would call here.

"Hello," I said.

"Hello! This is Dick Purcell! First off, congrats on getting married, Secondly, I need you to over here as soon as possible!"

"Excuse me Mr. Purcell," I replied, "but what do you mean by here? And you seem awfully excited. Please calm yourself."

"I'm sorry," he said. "I mean here as in my daughter's home. Someone has tried to harm her. Please come over and I'll explain once you get here." I looked around our house and decided to go. The chores had been done and our helpers were taking care of other needs.

"All right," I answered. "I'll be right over." Then I hung up. I gave instructions to the foreman and made sure our dogs were fine. I then decided to bring along Rory for safety. I leashed him up, jumped into my SUV, and drove off.

About 45 minutes later, I pulled alongside the curb of Lila Burns' house. I left the windows down slightly for my dog, got out, and rang the doorbell. The door opened and Mr. Burns was there.

"Oh, thank goodness you're here!" he exclaimed. "Come in." He led me into the living room. There I saw Lila, sitting with her father, and Sgt. Richards.

"What are you doing here, Sgt. Richards?" I asked.

"Josh got a call to come over but was busy and sent me instead. He also mentioned you'd probably show up."

"Hmm, so I did." I looked around, then asked what had happened.

"Please take a seat," Mr. Burns offered. Then he himself sat on his wife's other side.

Richards opened his mouth, but before he could say anything, Lila interrupted and said, "Please let me tell what happened." Richards nodded his head and she began her story.

"Mrs. Owens, somebody tried to kill me last night." To be honest, I was very concerned. She continued, "Robert was asleep, and I was awake thinking about everything that's happened. You see, I was with a friend the other day, and we were discussing all this dreadful business. I mentioned that I had been doing research and had just discovered something important. Also, that it tied into who the killer might be. I guess I shouldn't have been so public about it. Anyways, last night, I heard a noise down here and got up to make sure everything was okay. I came down but it was pitch dark. I thought I might have been hearing things when my mouth was suddenly gagged. I struggled to fight my attacker, but he pulled a gun to my head and told me to forget about the information that I had discovered or else Robert and I would get hurt. I was afraid and let myself go limp, then suddenly sprang at him. He took a shot but missed. Then he knocked me down and I blacked out." I was amazed.

Robert (Mr. Burns) then said, "I woke up because I thought I had heard something. I saw that my wife's bed was empty and became worried. I grabbed my revolver and came down. I saw our intruder and my wife was lying on the floor. I shouted and took a shot at him but missed. He ran out of the house and got away. After I took the gag out of Lila's mouth and laid her on the sofa, she told me what happened. Then I called up her dad and Richards." He stopped.

I was quiet for a second, then asked, "Can you describe him?"

"Mr. Burns said, "He was all in black, wore a mask, and about 5'10." Not much I'm afraid." I was thinking about the intruder, then asked Lila if there was anything else.

She looked at me, then said, "No, I was so afraid. And I didn't want anything to happen, especially in the condition that I'm in." We all looked at her quizzically.

"What condition?" asked her husband.

She grinned and exclaimed, "We're having a baby!"

Chapter 16

We all stared in amazement. Then everyone began to talk at once!

"Are you having a boy or girl?" asked Mr. Purcell.

"How far along are you?" I inquired.

"When's the baby due?" asked Richards.

"Wait till I tell Josh!" I exclaimed.

Robert still seemed spell-bound. "We're having a baby?" he asked incredulously.

"Whoaa! Everyone settle down," said Lila. "First, I don't know whether the baby's a boy or a girl. Secondly, I'm one month pregnant. Lastly, the baby is due July 4th. I have started to think of names, but nothing definite." She stopped and looked around, relieved to see we all were relaxed now.

"Well, I'll be leaving now," said Richards. With that, he got up, said goodbye, and left.

"I guess I'll be leaving too," I said. I smiled, nodded, then got up and let myself out into the cold. As I shut the front door, I looked down and noticed something snagged on one of the bushes. I bent down and examined what I'd found. I was elated! It turned out to be a piece of cloth which probably had been torn off the culprit's pants. I put the cloth into my pocket then stood up. I wanted to go home and tell Josh everything that had happened. At least it was a small lead.

I arrived home and realized I'd better start dinner. The chores were done, so after I whipped up a casserole and put it in the oven, I let out my dogs except Rory, who'd already been outside, then ushered them back in. I then took out the piece of cloth that I'd discovered earlier and examined it more closely with a magnifying glass. I really couldn't see much on the cloth. I put it in a small envelope and put that on the dinner table.

Finally, I was able to sit down on the sofa and relax, thinking about this mystery. Three murders and one attempted murder. This killer was getting bolder and more vicious. I wondered what would happen next. Would this killer take a new victim? Or will he decide to attack Lila again?

"Just what is his motive?" I said aloud.

"That's a good question. Find the killer, find the motive," responded a voice nearby. I looked up startled.

"Oh! Josh! I didn't hear you come in. I must have been so engrossed in trying to solve this case."

"That's okay," he said. "But how about a hug and a kiss?" He grinned. I got up and gave him a hug, laying my head on his chest, probably for a full three minutes. Then he put his hand under my chin, lifted my head up, and locked his lips onto mine. If there were any peeping toms, they would either be grossed out or would know that we were and still are deeply in love.

Well, we finally parted and I asked how his work had been.

"Oh, nothing special. The usual work, going through papers and files, when not actively on a case."

"I'm sorry it wasn't exciting. Why don't you relax now while I get dinner? It should be ready by now." Josh took off his shoes, lay down his briefcase, hung up his jacket, and sat down on the sofa. I went into the kitchen and took out my casserole from the oven. Thankfully, it was done and I dished it out onto plates along with some potatoes. I carried them out to our table, then came back to fetch the drinks.

I was glad that I only had to cook for Josh and myself. Our workers on the farm lived in a bunkhouse on the property which had a small kitchen with food, a bathroom, and other amenities-so it wasn't really just a bunkhouse. I sat down at the dinner table, and so did Josh. We said our prayer of thanks for the food, then began to eat. I explained to Josh all that had happened at Mrs. Burns' house and what had happened to her.

The only remark Josh made was, "This killer is getting desperate." Well, until I told him Lila was having a baby. Then he just stared in amazement, surprised, and said, "Well, congrats to her!"

After dinner, I cleared the dishes; then we talked for a while. The day ended and we went to bed. It wasn't as eventful as I wished it had been; as I drifted off to sleep, I realized I'd forgotten to show Josh the piece of cloth I'd found.

"Guess it'll have to wait till tomorrow," I thought. Then I fell asleep.

Chapter 17

The next morning, after I woke up, ate breakfast, and did the farm chores, I remembered the piece of cloth and decided to drive down to Josh's work office to show it to him. Lately, it seemed that I'd been getting slightly forgetful. Anyways, I tidied up the house, then hopped into my SUV and drove off. For some reason, I wasn't feeling myself. However, I pushed the feeling away, knowing that I couldn't afford to get sick now. I drove the rest of the way without incident and finally pulled into an empty parking space. I got out and went inside the 20-story building. Josh's office was on the 15th floor and I wasn't about to take the stairs, so I took the elevator. It seemed like it was taking forever for the elevator to reach the 15th floor. Of course, it was only a few minutes, and once the doors opened, I rushed out, accidentally bumping into Sgt. Richards.

"Emily! What are you doing here?" he asked in surprise.

"Oh, um, I have to tell Josh something. New evidence I just discovered. I'm hoping Josh can make sense of it." I smiled. "So, please excuse me; I must get going." With that, I quickly walked away and around the corner. I stopped, peeked out from my hiding spot, and saw Richards looking very bewildered. Then he muttered something and proceeded in the opposite direction. I was relieved and embarrassed-Richards probably was surprised by the way I had just acted, and frankly I was surprised too. I wasn't too sure why I had acted so skittish and cautious around Sgt. Richards. I knew him well so there was no reason to be that way. I figured maybe I was being overprotective about this new found clue and didn't want anything happening to it. Plus, the fact that I was still feeling off-not myself.

"Oh well," I thought. "I better be more careful and less skittish." Then I walked down the carpeted hallway and found Josh's office. I opened the door and went inside.

"Mrs. Owens, how are you doing?" asked Josh's secretary, Mrs. Scott. Mrs. Anne Scott was a widow and like a mother to Josh and me.

"I'm fine," I said. "Is Josh in?"

"He is, but there's some man speaking with him right now. However, I can announce you if you want."

"No, it's fine. I don't mind waiting." I went over and sat in a nearby chair.

A couple minutes later, the door to Josh's office opened and out stepped a man that I was truly surprised to see. It was Inspector Carol! I hadn't seen him since Susie Blackwell had been murdered. Come to think of it, that was quite some time ago, and I started to wonder just why he was now at Josh's office. I never did like him nor did anyone else. I didn't trust him either. As he passed by me, he stiffened but gave a slight smile.

"How are you doing Miss Randall?" I tried not to be furious.

"I'm fine, thanks. But it's Mrs. Owens for your information. I'm married now." Inspector Carol did not look pleased when he heard that. But then why should he even care? I mean I didn't understand how our marriage could in any way affect him. Anyways, I waited for a response.

"Oh, Mrs. Owens, I'm sorry. I didn't know you married. My apologies." Did that sound sarcastic? It did to me. I wondered why he seemed so unhappy.

"Oh, it's fine." I smiled. He looked at me with an expression on his face that I couldn't figure out, but it did send shivers up my spine. I finally got up and stepped into my husband's office.

"Emily, what brings you here?" asked Josh. He shut the door, then pulled up a chair for me. Before I could sit down, the room started to go in circles! I grabbed Josh to steady myself. "Are you okay? Darling, what's wrong?" He looked concerned.

"Oh! I just felt a little dizzy, that's all. I'm all right now." I slowly sat down.

"Maybe you've been focusing too hard on this case. Are you sick?"

"I'm not sure. I don't think so, but I haven't been feeling very well lately, and today has been much worse." I frowned. Josh took my hand. "What was Inspector Carol doing here?" I inquired. Josh's concerned look turned into a frown.

"Being a nuisance if you ask me. He wanted to know if we suspected who the killer might be, what and if we have any evidence, how far along we've come, etc." I raised my eyebrows.

"Why did he want to know that? What did you say? Isn't that a little suspicious? I mean he just appeared out of the blue and is asking questions. He gave me a weird look. I really don't trust him."

"I know" said Josh. "I refused to tell him anything; only that we've made some progress, but that we don't have a clue to the killer. I was on guard the whole time, and he seemed to be on guard as well. But enough about him-what brings you here?" I pulled out the piece of cloth from the envelope it was in.

"I found this yesterday when I was visiting Mrs. Burns. It was caught on the bush outside her house. I believe it's a torn piece from the killer's pants." I handed Josh the cloth. He examined it thoroughly, then put it down.

"Not much information I could get out of this. But what we can do is search for the pants that would match this missing piece." Suddenly, we heard a thump against the door. Then a voice started to shout and I knew something was amiss.

"Get yourself out of this room this instant or I'll whack you with this broom!" I jumped up and Josh sprang to the door and yanked it open! There, stood Mrs. Scott, broom in hand, ready to bring it down menacingly on—Inspector Carol!

Chapter 18

I t was a very amusing sight indeed. I almost blurted out "Let'm have it!" but I did not. Instead, I just grinned slightly, then turned serious. Josh was not happy at all; he was furious.

"What are you doing here Inspector Carol?" he asked sternly. Inspector Carol looked up, for he was shorter than Josh by a good six inches.

"Oh, I, um, just came back to see if I could find my tie clip. It, um, fell off somehow, and I thought I lost it here." Inspector Carol stopped and stood quiet. Personally, I couldn't help think how fake his story sounded. Mrs. Scott opened her mouth, probably to make a rebuttal to that falsehood of his. However, Josh interrupted her and spoke before anyone else could.

"Well, did you find it?" he asked, one eyebrow raised.

"Oh, yes, I did find it. Yes, I'll be going now," he stammered. With that, he walked quickly to the door of the waiting room and left, shutting the door behind him. Both Mrs. Scott and I looked at Josh questioningly.

"Why did you let him leave like that? You didn't believe his story, did you?" I asked.

"No; I didn't. But I did not want him to think that we suspect him of anything, and I wasn't sure that I wanted any problems just yet. I know he was eavesdropping." Josh gave a frown.

"He sure was!" exclaimed Mrs. Scott. "Why, I had to leave my desk to go out and run a quick errand. That snoop must have seen me leave. He must've come in here and listened to your conversation. I came back and saw him listening in, so I grabbed the broom and told him to scram. You know the rest." I was concerned.

"Josh, how much do you think he overheard?"

"I'm not sure, but he must have had a reason for eavesdropping."

I furrowed my brows, then asked, "Do you think that since he couldn't get any information out of you, he decided to find a way and listen in, hoping to hear something of interest?"

"That could be," replied Josh. "I wonder why, unless he actually has a connection in this whole case."

"Maybe, he had something to do with the murders. Or he was told and paid to eavesdrop. I wonder if he might have an accomplice." I looked at Josh expectantly.

"It wouldn't surprise me now. But why didn't we think of him before? He did disappear from the picture and now has reappeared suddenly," said Josh.

"Well, whatever he's up to and whomever he is, I won't let that no good varmint in here again!" exclaimed Mrs. Scott. "Now I have more work to do." She sat down at her desk and started typing.

Josh picked up his briefcase and keys, and put on his coat. "I'm not taking any chances. I will go home with you for today. Mrs. Scott, after you finish here, you may lock up and have the rest of the day off." Then he took me by the hand and we left. Since we had two cars, we each drove one home. Once home, Josh had me relax while he did some chores, let out the dogs, and even made some food. I, on the other hand, was sitting on the sofa, feeling dizzy again. I even was feeling worse than before.

Josh came out from the kitchen, then rushed over. "Honey, are you feeling okay? You look so pale!" Pale-well, I hadn't known that. "Emily, you'd better stay in bed today. I'll take care of everything." He lifted me up, carried me upstairs, and laid me on the bed.

"I'm ok, but I'm not feeling that well, if you want to know the truth."

"I can see that," said Josh. "Will you be all right here?"

"I'm sure I'll be fine. I'll just rest." I stretched out, and Josh seemed satisfied, so he went downstairs. I got up and changed into pajamas, then got under the covers. I was feeling very exhausted, but I wasn't sure why.

I must have slept for several hours because when I woke up, it was evening. I felt refreshed though, so that was good. I got up and went downstairs. Josh was writing something on a piece of paper. He looked up and was relieved to see me looking better.

"Feeling better?" he asked.

"Yes, much better," I said. "Just needed some extra sleep I guess." I sat down on the sofa, and Josh sat beside me.

"I think you ought to see the doctor tomorrow. Promise me you will go." He looked concerned.

"Ok, I promise. It might be good anyhow." I smiled. I stayed up a little later then Josh, planning the next day. Yes, I'd go to the doctor, but I had this feeling that I should go buy a pregnancy kit. That I would do tomorrow morning. For now, I would go to sleep and forget about the case, which was nearly impossible.

The next morning, I went out and bought the kit. Once back home, I used it. I needed to know whether or not my suspicions were correct. To my excitement, they were and I tested positive! I was pregnant! I was so happy and excited to tell Josh, but I also had other things to do. After chores, I got ready and drove to my doctor. From there, we figured out the next steps and the planning for these next upcoming months. After this, I debated on whether to wait for Josh to come home or to go to his office. I decided to wait. Then, as my mind wondered to the previous day's events, I thought of a daring plan. Well, not that daring. I was going to find out where Inspector Carol lived, go there, and if he wasn't home, sneak in and search for any pants that might be torn. Josh had left the cloth with me, so after lunch, I called his office and left a message with Mrs. Scott, letting him know where I'd be. It was easy to find Inspector Carol's address. Once I found it, I drove over there.

I parked a little ways off, and went up the rest of the way by foot. I looked around and saw no one or at least no cars in the driveway. I peered through a front window into the house and it seemed no one was home. "This might be trespassing, but if he's our killer, then this must be done," I thought. I put on gloves that I'd brought with me and was careful not to leave behind footprints. I looked for a way to get in, but there was none. Then I had an idea. I called up Agatha and asked her for help. She finally consented and drove to his house. When we met up, I grabbed her and we hid in the nearby bushes. I didn't know when our suspect would return home and I wasn't about to get trapped in his house. We'd just have to wait for him to come home, then get him out of the house. Hopefully, we wouldn't have to wait for long.

Chapter 19

Inspector Carol did not disappoint us. In about 15 minutes, he pulled into his driveway, got out, and went inside his house.

"How'd you know he would show up?" asked Agatha.

"I didn't. It was a guess," I answered. Then I continued, "Now, I want you to go to his house, knock on the door, and ask for Inspector Carol. He doesn't know you. Play your part well, maybe act like a young woman who's upset and needs to talk to someone. If necessary, and this is your last option, use your feminine wiles; flirt-be a little flirtatious. Shouldn't be too difficult for you."

"Emily, you're joking. I'll do it, but what about you?"

"I'll get in somehow and search for the torn pants, if they haven't been thrown away. If you can get him away from the house, then I could sneak in and search. Buy some time-maybe 20 minutes. If something happens and I get trapped, head for my husband's office or call him up and get Sgt. Richards. I'm confident Inspector Carol is our killer, but I need proof." I stopped.

"But Emily, that means he's dangerous, and we might get caught, or you will for trespassing."

"I know," I admitted, "but this is a chance we just have to take. We can't let more people become his victims."

"All right," sighed Agatha. "Here goes nothing." She came out of hiding and went up to the door. I saw her ring the bell, then wait. She was pretending to look distraught. The door opened and I witnessed the dialogue that took place.

"Hello, who are you?" demanded Inspector Carol.

"Oh! Are you Lewis Carol? Remember me, Aggie, well-I guess you wouldn't. It's been so long, but we used to date! Why haven't you gotten in touch with me darling? I missed you so much! Say you remember me…"

Inspector Carol stood there stunned. "Excuse me miss, but you're mistaken. I don't know you and we've never dated."

"How could you say such a thing!" And Agatha slapped him across the face. "Aren't you Lewis Carol? I mean I heard somewhere that you became an Inspector, but you'll always be my Lewis, my darling Lewis…" Agatha trailed off.

Inspector Carol was a bit shocked at having just been slapped in the face by someone he was sure he didn't know. "Sure, my first name's Lewis but that's nothing to you. I tell you I don't know you! What part of that do you not understand!?" Agatha was acting pretty well, for she started to shed a few tears. I guessed she was pretending to be genuinely upset at being forgotten.

Inspector Carol just stood there impatiently waiting for Agatha's response. I was surprised that he didn't just shut the door in her face. Then all of a sudden, and unexpectedly, Agatha threw herself into his arms. That definitely took him by surprise and me for that matter. Inspector Carol tried to get her off but to no avail. She clung tight, then let go. I just rolled my eyes.

"Well, you're just as handsome as you were some years ago. Wish I could jog your memory-we were such a cute couple! I don't blame you for not remembering me…but we can rekindle some of that old flame…" Agatha looked at him with those sad puppy eyes. "Why don't we go out right now!? You shouldn't be here alone you tough, handsome man." Agatha then batted her eyelashes.

"Good grief!" I thought. "She's overdoing it, but if she can get him to leave, and if I can get inside, then it'll be worth it."

"Um, I'm kind of busy right now; I mean, I'd like to take you out but uh—" he was cut off.

"Oh, swell! Come on then! We'll take my car, and we'll have a blast! I'm so glad you remember your sweet Aggie," cooed Agatha. She dragged him to her car. I was amused.

"Wait, I have to lock up first," insisted the Inspector.

"Oh, your house will be fine."

"Nevertheless," he said, "I shall lock up." He went back, locked the door, and put the keys in his pocket. Agatha seemed to be frustrated. Now she needed to get the key off so I could get in without actually breaking in. in one last effort, she tried again, and I must say that this time she went too far. She gave Inspector Carol a hug and started to flatter him some more. A little too much because he really did fall for it. It looked like that they were going to kiss. Then I saw Agatha reach her hand and pull out the keys quietly. Then she kept whispering to him while taking the house key off the chain and tossed it into the grass a ways off. Then she put the other keys back into his pocket. I thought for sure she would kiss him but she didn't and let go. Then she dragged him off, got into the car, and drove off. Finally, they were gone.

I got out of hiding, put on gloves so as not to leave any fingerprints, picked up the key, and unlocked the door. I went straight up the stairs to his bedroom since that'd be the most logical place to look for pants. I searched his closet and drawers but with no luck.

"Where are those pants?" I said out loud. I looked in his laundry basket but found no torn pants. Then, I had an idea and checked the trash cans inside and outside the house. Sure enough, I found a pair of pants that were torn in one of the indoor trash cans. Evidently, he was trying to get rid of them, but not in a smart way. I took them out and looked them over to be sure of the match with the torn piece of cloth I'd found a few days ago. And sure enough, it was a match! I was elated! I snapped pictures of it with my small camera. I put the pants back and straightened up the mess I'd made.

I went downstairs and headed towards the door, then stopped as I heard a car drive up. Footsteps sounded towards the door. I peeked out and saw Agatha's car, no Agatha, and Inspector Carol trying to find his house key on his chain. Then he lifted a flowerpot, put his hand in the dirt, and pulled out a key. Just my luck! I was trapped, and unless I could escape another way, I was in a bad spot. I went and hid in a closet. The door opened and Inspector Carol walked in. He stopped. All was quiet; then all of a sudden, the closet door was yanked open!

Inspector Carol pulled me out and sneered at me, "So, you decided to snoop! Well, it's over for you! I caught on to your little scheme and I took care of your friend."

"If you harmed her, I'll—"

"Now, now," he cut in abruptly, "she's not hurt. But she's tied up and will freeze where she's at now."

"What do you plan to do—kill me like you killed all the others?"

"Quiet! You know too much!" That was the last I heard. Everything went black, and before I became totally unconscious, I realized that I must have been knocked out from behind.

Chapter 20

My head was spinning, my eyes and brain felt groggy. It took several minutes for me to become fully aware of my surroundings. Once I was consciously aware, I looked around and noticed that I couldn't move my head as much. It was pitch dark all around me and I felt a weight on top of me. As a matter of fact, I had trouble moving my whole body. It seemed as if I was trapped in some enclosed space. I finally was able to force my arms into movement but not much. I pushed up with my arms and felt something above me, or more like on me. I shuddered as I realized that the shape of what I felt weighing me down was a body! My adrenaline started to rush and I was frantic. A dead body lying on top of me could only mean one thing-I was inside a coffin. That meant I could suffocate and time was ticking by quickly.

I wasn't sure how long I'd been inside, but I knew I wouldn't have long until my body would give out, or succumb to the sleep of no return. I tried to move around the body and push open the top but to no avail. Then I wondered about Agatha and realized that she'd be my only hope if nothing else had happened to her. I really hoped she'd come to the rescue. It was already getting stifling warm in here and air was running thin. I was feeling faint and realized I'd better put everything in God's hands. I tried once more to push open the door, but again to no avail. I tried to keep my eyes open, to stay conscious, there just seemed no hope. I finally just relaxed and started to lose consciousness when I started to hear voices and running footsteps. Then I lost all consciousness.

I slowly opened my eyes, shut them, then reopened them. For a while, I was disoriented. I looked around and saw all these people standing around me. It finally clicked in my mind as to who they all were. I noticed there were quite a few doctors, nurses, and some officers standing around. Then I saw Sgt. Richards and to my relief, Agatha next to him. Then I realized that Josh was present and holding my hand. I was speechless, knowing now that I was in the hospital, and that Agatha had escaped and was safe. Finally, I spoke up.

"What happened? Josh, what's going on?"

"It's all right, dear. You're safe now. When you feel ready, tell us what happened." I relaxed, shut my eyes, sighed, then began my story.

"Well, Josh, the day after you took me home, I had to run an errand. After that, I had lunch, then thought about what you said about finding those torn pants. I suspected Inspector Carol and went to his house. I got Agatha to come help and she used her feminine wiles and wit to get Inspector Carol out. She left me the key, which she got off the key chain, and I then searched his house. I found the pants in a trash can but Inspector Carol came back abruptly and sooner than I'd expected. I knew something was up; I hid in a closet and he came in with a spare key. However, he apparently knew I was there and opened the closet door. He dragged me out, threatened me, and must have had a confederate because next thing I knew, someone conked me from behind. I also had learned Agatha had been tied up and left to freeze somewhere. Well, the next thing that I remembered is that I woke up inside a coffin with a dead body on top of me. I heard voices and footsteps right before I lost consciousness. I think when I was knocked out, I was dragged somewhere afterwards. Anyways, Inspector

Lewis Carol is the man you want and whomever his confederate is as well. After my time in the coffin, I woke up here. Now,
maybe you could fill in the gaps." Josh looked grim.

"We know about Lewis Carol and his confederate, who goes by
the name of Butch Brady. Unfortunately, they escaped but officers
are on their trail right now. Agatha was tied up in a shed, but she
managed to free herself and hailed a cab. She witnessed the two
men drag you out of the house. You were out cold and drugged
so you wouldn't wake up. They put you in Lewis Carol's car and
drove off. Agatha had taken that cab to his house, then switched
to her car and followed the two men for a while. She saw them
enter a funeral home, drove off to get the police, then called me
and Richards. By the time we got there, your abductors were gone,
but officers picked up their trail. We went inside and searched
the place. The person in charge was in cahoots with them and
was arrested. We found a casket that was sealed shut. We pried it
open and discovered you, with a body on top-which had been dug
up from its grave so they could put both of you in the ground, in
other words bury you. We got you out and here to the hospital.
You were very near death. Fortunately, doctors and nurses were
able to save you." I was shocked to hear it all together now.

"Ma'am, I'm Dr. Harris," an older man with gray hair said,
stepping forward, "and yes, you nearly died, but by God's grace
you are still with us." I was relieved, to be honest. Dr. Harris
then smiled at me and Josh. "Your wife has good news for you.
But I'll let her tell you." Josh looked confused. I grinned.

"Darling, we're going to have a baby!" Josh's eyes widened,
and I can't describe the look of joy on his face. Just then, an
officer came in pulled Richards aside for a little bit. Then,
Richards came over to us and he seemed happy.

"You'll be glad to know Lewis Carol and Butch Brady have
been apprehended and are behind bars now. It seems the
motive was money and revenge. Carol knew Susie Blackwell,
even had a relationship with her but then ended up wanting

her estate. He hoped to marry her but she spurned him. It was all for money and revenge. He never really cared for her, just her estate and money. If she died, he could inherit. But that didn't happen. A few years passed, and he learned of her and Wilbur. He didn't like Wilbur, who was suspicious of him. He thought Wilbur would get in the way of everything. He also thought that Susie's daughter was Wilbur's and not Dick's. He hadn't realized Dick and Susie had been married.

Carol hated Wilbur so he did away with him after killing Susie and Rachel. Susie was killed as I said, for money and revenge. He let himself in when no one was around and planted the poison hemlock in her salad. When the maid mentioned that she thought she'd heard a man speaking with Susie in the den, it was really Carol speaking with her; however, the maid was around to hear only Wilbur's name mentioned by Carol. Rachel knew something was up and saw a picture of the plant that was used in the salad. She recognized it as poison hemlock but was too late in revealing what she'd discovered since Carol found out what she knew, confronted her, and killed her. Then of course, Wilbur got suspicious and had been for a while and even confronted Carol. Carol's accomplice was responsible for killing Wilbur but under command of Carol the day following the confrontation. Also, the day we were in Susie's house and the lights went out, that was his accomplice that did that. It was to cause confusion and scare us. He and an accomplice went over to Lila's house to scare her but that was thwarted; while rushing to get out of her house, Carol accidentally snagged his pants against the bush. He had overheard Lila say to a friend that she'd discovered something that might be linked to who the killer was. He didn't want to be found out. That's the whole of it."

I just sat there in amazement wondering how people could be so cruel. Well, one thing I knew for certain was that revenge doesn't pay. Of course, I was also looking forward to having a family of three.

About the Author

Abigail Fucci was born in England and currently resides in Virginia with her family. She graduated from Seton Catholic High School in 2018 and is currently a senior studying clinical psychology at Franciscan University of Steubenville in Ohio, expecting to graduate December 2021. She loves spending time with friends, family, and her nephews and nieces and thanks God for everything. She became interested in writing after her English class during junior year of high school and now enjoys writing poetry and public speaking. She loves fury animals, the color red, making potholders, reading, bowling, and swimming in the summer. She is a huge mystery fan and loves watching murder mysteries with her mom. Her main goal regarding graduating college is to go where the Lord takes her. She would like to become a full-time mother in the future when God decides it's right. She also loves old country music and country gospel along with anything Christian. Her message to you is that no matter how you feel and what suffering you're going through, you still have purpose and meaning-don't give up!

CPSIA information can be obtained
at www.ICGtesting.com
Printed in the USA
BVHW031443100921
616516BV00005B/611